My Secret Unicorn

A Touch of Magic

'All animals can talk. People just need to listen.'
What did she mean? Animals couldn't talk.
Well, apart from Twilight, and that was
only because he was a unicorn.
'I just don't get it,' she said as she groomed
Twilight a little while later. 'Animals can't talk.
What did Mrs Fontana mean?'

My Secret Unicorn

A Touch of Magic

Linda Chapman

Illustrated by Ann Kronheimer

PUFFIN

PUFFIN BOOKS

UK | USA | Canada | Ireland | Australia
India | New Zealand | South Africa

Puffin Books is part of the Penguin Random House group of companies
whose addresses can be found at global.penguinrandomhouse.com.

www.penguin.co.uk   www.puffin.co.uk   www.ladybird.co.uk

Penguin
Random House
UK

First published 2005
This edition published 2018

005

Written by Linda Chapman
Text copyright © Working Partners Ltd, 2005
Illustrations copyright © Ann Kronheimer, 2005
Created by Working Partners Ltd, London W6 0QT

The moral right of the author and illustrator has been asserted

Typeset in 14.25/21.5 pt Bembo
Printed in Great Britain by Clays Ltd, Elcograf S.p.A.

A CIP catalogue record for this book is available from the British Library

ISBN: 978-0-241-37086-5

All correspondence to:
Puffin Books
Penguin Random House Children's
80 Strand, London WC2R 0RL

To Holly and Charlotte Allison

CHAPTER
One

Three strides, two strides, one stride . . .
Twilight soared through the air
and landed safely on the other side of the
jump.

'Good boy!' Lauren Foster exclaimed,
patting his neck. Mel and Jessica, Lauren's
two best friends clapped from where they
were sitting on their ponies, Shadow and
Sandy. The three girls had spent an hour

after school putting up a course of jumps in the field at Mel's farm.

'It's like he's flying!' Mel called.

Lauren bit back a grin. If only Mel knew her secret! Even though Twilight looked like an ordinary pony most of the time, when Lauren said some magic words, he turned into a snow–white unicorn who actually *could* fly. The only people who knew the truth were an old lady called Mrs Fontana and Lauren's friend Michael, who lived in the city and had a secret unicorn pony of his own.

Lauren pointed Twilight towards the final fence. Mel had decided to put a row of flowerpots in front, which made it look enormous.

Lauren gulped. Suddenly she wasn't so sure about jumping it. *What if Twilight fell . . .?*

Twilight slowed down.

Lauren clicked her tongue, but Twilight got slower still. He was going to refuse! Lauren forced down her fear. 'Come on, Twilight!' she cried, pressing him on. Twilight sped up again and they flew over it.

'Good boy!' Lauren gasped as they landed safely.

'That was great,' Mel said as Lauren trotted over.

'I didn't think I was going to make the last fence,' Lauren replied. 'Twilight slowed down a lot.'

Mel frowned. 'That's not like Twilight. He hasn't hurt himself, has he?'

Lauren felt a flicker of alarm. 'I don't know.' Dismounting, she checked Twilight's legs. There were no obvious cuts or grazes. She picked up his hooves, but they were clear of stones. 'He seems all right.'

'Maybe it was just the jump that made him slow down,' Jessica suggested. 'It *is* really big.'

'Yeah,' Lauren agreed. 'Those flower pots make it look huge.' She noticed that the sun had started to set beyond the mountains that rose up in the distance. 'I'd better go. Are we going to meet up tomorrow and do our school project?'

'Definitely,' said Mel. 'We've still got loads to do. We've got to make our project the best!'

For the last few days, their class at school had been working in groups. They'd had to choose a hobby to talk about and the following week they were going to present their talks to the class. Lauren, Mel and Jessica had naturally decided to do their project on ponies.

'I wish Jade's and David's groups weren't doing horse riding as well,' Jessica sighed.

Mel nodded. 'The people who aren't into ponies are going to get really bored listening to three talks about the same thing.'

'We'll just have to think of some way to make our project different,' Lauren said. 'We can do that tomorrow.' She

squeezed Twilight on. 'See you guys in
the morning.'

As Lauren rode Twilight up the drive
that linked Mel's farm with the road, the
last few rays of the sun glowed on
Twilight's mane. 'You were great today,'
Lauren told him. Then she remembered
how he had slowed down at the last
jump. 'You are OK though, aren't you?
You're not hurt?'

Twilight snorted.

Lauren wondered
what a snort meant.
She knew Twilight
understood every
word she said, but he
could only talk back

to her when he was a unicorn. She felt
slightly alarmed. Maybe there *was*
something wrong and he was trying to
tell her!

They reached the end of the drive.
Lauren normally turned right towards
Granger's Farm, where she lived with her
mum, dad and younger brother, Max. But
now she hesitated. There was a wooded
area on the other side of the road. If she
rode into the trees she could turn
Twilight into a unicorn and ask him if
there was anything wrong.

She checked the road. It was empty.
'Come on, Twilight,' she whispered. 'I'm
going to turn you into a unicorn.'

They entered the trees. Once they were

hidden from sight, Lauren jumped off
Twilight's back and said the magic words
of the Turning Spell:

> *'Twilight Star, Twilight Star*
> *Twinkling high above so far.*
> *Shining light, shining bright,*
> *Will you grant my wish tonight?*
> *Let my little horse forlorn*
> *Be at last a unicorn!'*

There was a bright purple flash and
suddenly Twilight was no longer a scruffy
grey pony. Instead he had transformed
into a beautiful unicorn with a snowy
coat and a gleaming silver horn in the
centre of his forehead.

'Twilight!' Lauren exclaimed, hugging him.

Twilight tossed his silvery mane. 'Hi, Lauren.' His mouth didn't move but as long as Lauren was either touching him or holding a hair from his mane she could hear him speaking as clearly as if he was another human being.

'Are you OK?' Lauren asked anxiously.
'Why did you slow down at that last
fence?'

'It felt like you didn't really want to
jump it,' Twilight replied. 'As we were
going towards it, you pulled on the reins
and stopped pressing me on. I didn't want
to jump if you were frightened.'

Lauren remembered the way her
stomach had somersaulted when she had
turned into the fence. 'I guess I was
scared for a few seconds,' she admitted.
'I'm sorry I pulled on your mouth.'

'That's OK,' Twilight replied, rubbing
his ears against her while being careful
not to catch her with his horn. 'You
didn't pull hard.'

Lauren gave him a hug. She was very relieved to find out that he wasn't hurt. 'I'd better turn you back now,' she told him. 'Mum and Dad will be wondering where I am. But I'll come to your field later and we can go flying.'

She said the words of the Undoing Spell and Twilight turned back into a pony.

Lauren mounted and rode out of the trees. As Twilight's hooves clip-clopped along the quiet road, she thought how lucky she was to be able to talk to him. It meant she could always find out if there was anything wrong. She felt her heart swell with love. She had a secret unicorn of her own! Oh yes, she was very lucky indeed.

Two

'You've been riding late,' said Lauren's dad as Lauren walked into the kitchen a little while later.

'Mel, Jessica and I were jumping,' Lauren explained, sitting down to pull off her boots. Buddy, Max's dog, trotted over to say hello. He was a young Bernese mountain dog and almost as big as a small Shetland pony. He plonked his heavy head in her lap and Lauren stroked him. 'Where's Mum?' she asked.

'Working in her study,' her dad replied. 'I said I'd fix supper tonight.'

Lauren's mum was a writer and she often shut herself in her study for hours at a time when she was trying to finish a book.

Mr Foster stirred some pasta into a pan of boiling water on the stove. 'So, it's Saturday tomorrow. What're you up to? Are you seeing Mel and Jessica?'

'Yes,' Lauren replied, scratching Buddy's ears. 'We're doing a project together on our favourite hobby. We've got to give a talk in front of the whole class.' She frowned. 'I just hope it's interesting enough, Dad. Two other groups are doing their projects on horses too.'

'I'm sure you'll think of something to make your project stand out,' Mr Foster said comfortingly.

'I hope so,' Lauren sighed.

Buddy wriggled around so he was sitting on her feet. He pressed against Lauren's legs, his tail thumping. Lauren laughed. 'Buddy's being affectionate tonight.'

'I don't think Max has fed him yet.' Mr Foster went to the kitchen door. 'Max, come and feed Buddy please!'

'In a minute!' Lauren heard her six-year-old brother call back from the living room.

'Now,' Mr Foster insisted.

'What's Max doing?' Lauren asked.

'Watching some DVD about skateboarding,' Mr Foster replied. 'Steven and Leo lent it to him.'

Lauren nodded. Ever since Steven and Leo Vance had moved into a house just along the road, Max had been really into skateboarding. Leo and Steven who were eight and ten years old, both had skateboards and Max had been going round to play with them at the weekends and after school.

Max came into the kitchen looking grumpy. 'It was just at a really good bit, Dad.'

Mr Foster shrugged. 'Sorry, Max, but

Buddy needs feeding. DVDs can wait. Animals can't.'

Max sighed but fetched Buddy's bowl. With his curly brown hair and brown eyes he looked just like a smaller version of their dad.

'Is it a good DVD?' Lauren asked him.

Max's eyes lit up. 'It's great! It shows

you how to do all these jumps. Leo and
Steven can do loads of them and I'm
going to learn too. I did a proper Ollie
today!'

'Oh . . . that's good,' Lauren said, not
having a clue what an Ollie was.

'I'm going over to their house
tomorrow to practise some more.' Max
put Buddy's bowl of food down.

'Maybe you should invite Leo and
Steven over here, Max,' Mr Foster
suggested. 'You always seem to be going
to their house.'

'That's because they've got a proper
place to skate,' Max replied. 'They've got
a launch ramp *and* a quarter pipe to
practise on.'

'Well, we could make something here,' Mr Foster said. 'You could use that concreted area near Twilight's field – the place where the old barn was. I could construct you a ramp or two.'

Max looked at him in delight. 'Really?'

Mr Foster nodded. 'I'll see what I can do. However, I don't want to see you forgetting Buddy's supper again, Max. Having a pet is a big responsibility. You have to think of his needs before your own.'

'I'll feed Buddy on time from now on, I promise,' Max said happily. He stroked Buddy. 'Sorry, boy.' Buddy looked up from licking his bowl clean and wagged his tail.

Mr Foster smiled. 'OK, you can go and watch some more of your DVD. But only ten minutes and then it's supper time.'

Max ran out of the room. Lauren watched him go. She couldn't understand his new craze for skateboarding. It seemed to be all he was interested in at the moment.

Buddy came over and she stroked him.
Her dad was right. Since Max had started
skateboarding he hadn't been spending
nearly as much time with Buddy as he
used to. Lauren could feel tangles in the
thick white fur around Buddy's collar.
When had Max last brushed him? She
wasn't sure. Bending down, she kissed the
overgrown puppy. She hoped Max was
going to start paying him some more
attention soon.

That night, when her parents had gone to
bed, Lauren crept out to Twilight's field.
He was waiting by the gate.

Lauren wasted no time. She whispered
the words of the Turning Spell and

Twilight became a unicorn once again.

'Sorry I'm late,' Lauren said. 'Mum and Dad stayed up later than usual.' She scrambled on to Twilight's warm back. 'Let's go flying!'

Twilight whinnied in delight and plunged into the sky. They flew up and up. Lauren's long fair hair blew back from her face but she felt wrapped in warmth. Twilight's magic meant she never felt cold when they were flying – and she never felt tired afterwards. Twilight could do all kinds of magic – special magic to help other people or animals in danger. He could heal wounds, make people feel brave, cut a path through snow and see things that were happening far away. He

had other powers too – powers that he
and Lauren were still finding out about.

Suddenly Twilight slowed down.
'Listen, Lauren! Can you hear that noise?
It sounds like an animal in trouble.'

Listening hard, Lauren heard it too. A
panicked squeaking noise was coming
from the ground beneath them. 'Quick!'
she said. 'Let's go and see what it is!'

Three

Twilight landed in a clearing.

'The noise is coming from over there,' he said, pointing with his horn to a tangle of prickly hawthorn at the edge of the clearing.

Jumping off Twilight's back, Lauren went to investigate. 'Look, Twilight!'

It was very dark but Lauren could see a baby squirrel was caught in the depths of

the thicket. Its thick bushy tail was
tangled up in thorns and it was struggling
desperately.

'Poor little thing!' Lauren exclaimed.
She flung herself down on her tummy
and pushed her arm through the thorny
branches. The squirrel's black eyes darted
around frantically.

'It's OK. I'm here to help you,' Lauren
soothed. 'Ow!' she cried as the thorns
raked down her arm.

'Here, let me help,' Twilight offered. He
bent down and started to push the bushes
aside with his horn.

There was a vivid purple flash and a
cloud of smoke. Lauren gasped and
Twilight snorted in surprise. Even the

squirrel stopped squeaking for a moment
and stared.

The long branches had started to
unwind from each other as if they had
come alive.

'The brambles, Twilight!' cried Lauren.
'They're untangling! It must be another
of your magic powers!' she breathed.

Soon, the brambles had untangled

completely and there was a clear pathway to the squirrel. Lauren edged closer. Hoping it wouldn't turn round and bite her, she gently released its tail from the prickly bramble.

It was free! Lauren wriggled back. The squirrel looked round at its tail and suddenly seemed to realize it was no longer trapped. It scampered out into the clearing and up a nearby tree. With a joyful flick of its tail, it vanished into the leaves.

Lauren smiled. 'It's going to be OK,' she said, putting her arm over Twilight's neck and giving him a hug. 'I'm glad we could help.'

'Me too,' he agreed.

Taking hold of his mane, Lauren swung herself on to his back. A glow of happiness spread inside her. Using Twilight's magic to help animals or people always felt great! 'Come on. Let's fly some more,' she said.

'OK,' Twilight replied eagerly.

Holding fast to his mane, Lauren laughed out loud as he plunged into the sky.

When Lauren woke up the next morning she didn't feel tired at all. She jumped out of bed and pulled on her clothes. She had the whole weekend in front of her!

'We're going to have fun this morning, Twilight,' she said happily as she brushed him after breakfast. 'When I've finished grooming you, we'll go to Mel's house and go riding and then you can go out in the field with Shadow and Sandy while Mel, Jess and I do our project.'

Twilight snorted.

Lauren heard the sound of Max giggling and looked round. He was dragging a large plank of wood across the concrete area next to Twilight's field. Buddy was gambolling around him, getting in his way.

'Get off, Buddy!' Max said, sounding half-exasperated, half-amused.

Lauren went over to the fence. 'What are you doing?'

'Setting up some stuff to make skateboard ramps. Dad's going to come out in a minute and help me.'

'Do you want a hand?'

'Yes, please,' Max replied.

Lauren climbed the fence and took one end of the heavy plank. Buddy bounded around in excitement, almost tripping Max over.

'Buddy! Stop it!' Max exclaimed.

As he lowered his end of the plank, Buddy banged into his legs. Max lost his grip and dropped the plank on his toe. 'Ow!' he cried, hopping up and down.

'Are you OK?' Lauren asked.

'Yeah,' her brother replied, rubbing his toe. 'Dumb dog!' Buddy whined.

'Buddy's not dumb. He was just trying to play,' Lauren protested. She looked at

the confused dog. Buddy wasn't normally
quite so wild. 'Have you taken him out
for a walk this morning?'

Max looked down, his cheeks turning
pink.

'Max?' Lauren questioned. 'You *have*
taken him for his morning walk, haven't
you?'

'Well . . . no,' Max admitted. 'I've been designing my new skateboard course since I got up. I haven't had time.'

'Max, you can't not walk him!' Lauren exclaimed. 'No wonder he's acting so crazy.'

'I'll do it later,' Max said. He went over to Buddy and took hold of his collar. 'Come on, Buddy. You can go in the house. You're just getting in the way.'

'Max . . .' Lauren started to protest.

Just then their dad came walking up to the gate. 'Hi, you two!' Seeing Max pulling Buddy by the collar, he frowned. 'What are you doing, Max?'

'Putting Buddy inside,' Max answered. 'I guess it'll be easier if he's out of our way,' Mr Foster agreed.

Lauren wondered what she should do. Her dad didn't know Buddy hadn't been walked that day. She didn't want to get her brother into trouble but he was being really unfair. 'Max,' she hissed. 'Buddy needs to have some exercise!'

Max ignored her and marched on.

'What time are you going to Mel's?' her dad called.

'Um . . . I said I'd be there at nine thirty,' Lauren said, turning to him.

'You'd better get a move on then,' Mr Foster pointed out.

Lauren headed across the field towards Twilight. 'Oh, Twilight, I don't know what to do,' she said when she reached him. 'I feel really sorry for Buddy but I don't want to tell Dad because then he'll be mad with Max.'

Twilight nudged at his empty feed bucket with his nose. Then he looked at her with his intelligent dark eyes.

Lauren frowned. 'Your bucket? Food?' Suddenly she worked out what he was trying to say. 'You mean I could give Buddy some food? That's a great idea! I could stuff some treats in his rubber toy. That should keep him busy. Thanks, Twilight!'

Twilight tossed his head and Lauren gave him a hug, thinking for the thousandth time how great it was to have a unicorn!

CHAPTER

Four

Getting the toy ready for Buddy made Lauren late but she didn't care. She felt much happier knowing that Buddy had something to do while he waited for Max.

Mel and Jessica were saddled up, waiting for her.

'Let's go for a ride in the fields,' Mel suggested.

The three girls rode down the farm
track. The sun was shining and the ponies
snorted eagerly, pulling at their bits.
Patting Twilight's smooth neck, and
looking at Sandy and Shadow's pricked
ears, Lauren felt a wave of happiness. It
was wonderful to be out riding with her
friends on such a lovely spring morning.
She couldn't think of anything she
would rather be doing, apart from flying,
of course!

When they got back from their ride,
Lauren, Mel and Jessica untacked the
ponies and turned them out.

'Where's Samantha this weekend?'
Lauren asked Jessica.

Samantha was Jessica's step-sister and they shared Sandy.

'She's visiting her dad,' Jessica replied. 'She's going to stay with him until tomorrow night.' She took off her hat and shook her short blonde hair. 'Shall we get started on the project?'

Lauren nodded and they went to find Mel, who was in the tack room.

'We can do the project over there,' Mel said, pointing to a large wooden chest where the horses' brushes and clean saddlecloths were kept. It was covered in sheets of paper, horse books and felt-tip pens. 'I thought we could do some big posters.'

'That's a great idea,' Lauren agreed. 'You could do some cartoons on them.'

They settled down to work. Lauren and Jessica made a poster showing the different colours and breeds of horses, and Mel made another with funny cartoon drawings showing how *not* to look after a pony. In one cartoon there was a rider facing the wrong way; in another, someone was trying to groom a pony with a vacuum cleaner.

'These posters look really good,' Jessica said admiringly, after an hour.

Mel nodded. 'I'm still worried about doing our talk last, though. You know what the boys in the class are like when they get bored. They'll probably start acting really dumb.'

They exchanged worried looks.

'It'll be fine,' Lauren said, trying to be optimistic. 'The other groups might not have cartoons.'

Looking slightly reassured, Mel and Jessica went back to work on the posters.

Lauren felt nervous. She'd better be right!

✳

At lunchtime, Lauren rode home. As she took Twilight to his stable she heard someone call her name. Her dad and Max were waving to her from the new skateboard area. It had been transformed. Where once there had been just concrete, there were now a low rail, a small ramp, a steeper ramp and a couple of milk crates arranged into a jump.

'What do you think, Lauren?' Mr Foster called.

'It looks really good,' Lauren replied.

'We've just finished,' her dad said. 'Max was about to try it out.'

'Watch me, Lauren! Watch!' Max insisted.

Putting his helmet on, he set off

around the course. He was slightly
wobbly on his skateboard, but he
managed to get up both the ramps and
back down, only falling off once. He even
tried a jump where the board stayed as if
glued to his feet while he was in the air.

'That's an Ollie,' he called proudly. 'I'm

going to practise and practise until I'm as good as Steven and Leo. I want to learn how to do a kick flip next. That's when the board flips as you jump.' His eyes shone.

Lauren smiled. 'That's great, Max.'

She rode Twilight over to the fence and

dismounted. 'I just don't get skateboarding at all,' she said quietly to him as she ran the stirrups up the leathers. 'I mean, so someone can jump and turn the board under their feet? What's the big deal?' She thought for a moment. 'I guess that's how some people must feel about riding horses,' she decided.

Untying Twilight, she turned him out. Then she began to rinse Twilight's feed buckets. It would be good to get them cleaned before she went inside.

'Come on, Max. Let's go get some lunch!' Mr Foster called.

Max and Mr Foster walked over to her. 'What did you think of my skating,

Lauren?' Max asked eagerly.

'It looked great,' Lauren told him, emptying the water out of one of the buckets. It formed a muddy puddle on the ground.

Max stroked his skateboard lovingly, brushing away some tiny specks of dust. 'I can't wait to tell Steven and Leo about my new ramps!'

Just then there was a loud woof and Buddy came charging down the path.

'Mum must have let Buddy out,' Mr Foster said. 'Steady, boy!' he called to the excited dog.

But Buddy took no notice. He charged straight up to Max, his enormous paws splashing into the muddy puddle.

'Buddy! No!' Max gasped.

Lauren leapt back just in time. Water went all over Max and his skateboard.

'Oh, Buddy!' Max yelled, looking at his muddy skateboard. 'Look what you've done!'

Five

Buddy sat down and thumped the tip of his tail uncertainly on the ground. 'I'm going to have to wash my skateboard now!' Max said crossly.

'It was an accident, Max,' said Mr Foster. 'Buddy didn't mean any harm. It's OK, Buddy.' Buddy jumped up and looked hopefully at Mr Foster. 'What is it, boy? You look like you want something.'

Buddy trotted forward and pushed his head against him.

'Max?' Mr Foster said suddenly. 'You have walked Buddy today, haven't you?'

'Um . . .' Max caught Lauren's eye. 'Well . . . not exactly,' he admitted. 'You see, I was busy and –'

'Max!' Mr Foster exclaimed. 'Poor Buddy. Go and take him for a walk right now.'

'But it's lunchtime!' Max protested.

'Well, you'll have to wait,' Mr Foster said firmly. 'Animals come first, and don't look at me like that,' he added as Max pulled a face. 'I'm very disappointed in you.'

'I'm sorry,' Max muttered. 'I suppose

I *should* have walked Buddy.'

Mr Foster nodded. 'Yes, you should.
You should take a leaf out of your sister's
book. She's always spending time with
Twilight, grooming him, feeding him,
noticing when there's something wrong.'
He smiled at her, but
Lauren felt a bit
awkward. Twilight was
easy to look after –
after all,

he could talk to her. And yes, she did spend a lot of time with him, but some of the time was when he was a unicorn. Her dad didn't know that!

'Go on, off you go,' Mr Foster said to Max. 'Lauren, are you coming in for lunch?'

Lauren hesitated. She felt sorry for Max. 'It's OK, Dad. I'll walk Buddy with Max.'

Max looked at her in surprise.

'OK,' Mr Foster shrugged. 'I'll see you both in the house when you get back.' He walked off.

'Dad's really annoying,' Max grumbled.

'He only told you off because he cares about Buddy,' she said as they set off down the path.

'Buddy's fine,' Max insisted.

'You *have* been neglecting him a bit,' Lauren ventured.

'I haven't!' Max said defensively. Buddy bounded over. 'See, he's happy.'

'Yes – now,' Lauren replied. 'But he looked really miserable this morning. You have to start paying him more attention, Max.'

'I do pay him attention!' Max protested. 'You're just fussing about nothing. Buddy's fine!'

'Yeah, right,' Lauren said. 'You forgot his supper yesterday, you didn't walk him today –'

'If you're going to nag me, I'll walk on

my own,' Max said sulkily.

Lauren sighed. 'OK, let's not argue.'
Buddy trotted up to her and she stroked
his head. 'Come on, let's play hide and
seek with Buddy.'

Max nodded, cheering up. 'I'll hide
first.'

Hide and seek was one of Buddy's
favourite games. Max and Lauren took it

in turns to hide for Buddy to find them. Then they had him jump over some low obstacles they made out of branches and fallen logs.

'This is fun!' Max exclaimed as he sprang over a small log with Buddy beside him.

'It is,' Lauren said, grinning.

After a while, they headed back to the farmhouse for lunch. Max was in a much better mood.

'Thanks for walking with me, Lauren,' he said. 'Sometimes it can be kind of lonely taking Buddy for walks.'

Lauren frowned. She hadn't thought about it before but it *must* be lonely for Max. She had Mel and Jessica to go riding with and even if they weren't there Twilight could talk to her if she turned him into a unicorn. Max didn't have *anyone* to talk to when he was walking Buddy.

'It's a pity you haven't got any friends with dogs nearby,' she said. 'What about Steven and Leo? Do they like dogs?'

Max shrugged. 'I don't know. We only ever talk about skateboarding.' The farmhouse came into sight. 'Come on!' he exclaimed. 'I'll race you. I'm starving!'

For the rest of the afternoon, Lauren kept thinking about what Max had said. It was no wonder he was spending so much time with Steven and Leo; they were the only boys who lived within walking distance of the farm. Lauren hadn't thought about Max being lonely before and she wished there was a way to help him out.

'Can you think of anything we could do, Twilight?' she asked that evening when she turned him into a unicorn.

Twilight looked thoughtful. 'Maybe Max could come out on his bike with Buddy when we ride in the woods?'

Lauren considered it. 'Yes, and we could go out for picnics together. If I did more with Max, he might look after Buddy better.' She felt more cheerful. 'I'll ask him to come for a walk tomorrow.'

'That's a good idea.' Twilight nuzzled her. 'Come on, let's go flying now!'

CHAPTER
Six

The following morning, Lauren found Max in the kitchen with Buddy. 'Would you like to do something with Buddy and Twilight this morning?' she suggested. 'We could go into the woods. You could ride your bicycle and I could ride Twilight.'

'OK,' Max said eagerly.

'We can go after breakfast,' Lauren said,

putting a piece of bread in the toaster.

'I've had my breakfast,' Max said. Just then, the phone rang. Max picked it up. 'Granger's Farm,' he answered. A smile spread across his face. 'Hi, Steven. Yeah, I'd love to come over. You'll never guess what – Dad and I have built some ramps here!' There was a pause. 'OK. I'll go and ask my mum if I can come now.'

Max put the phone down. 'That was Steven,' he explained. 'He's invited me over so I won't be able to come to the woods with you.'

The kitchen door opened and Mrs Foster came in. 'Mum! Can I go to Steven and Leo's?' Max asked.

'Sure,' Mrs Foster said. 'But you have to

walk Buddy first.'

'Oh . . .' Max started to complain but
he seemed to notice their mum's eyebrows
raise. 'OK,' he sighed. 'I'll do it now.'

'Make sure it's a proper walk,'
Mrs Foster added as he
pulled on his trainers. 'Dad
said you didn't walk him
yesterday

until lunchtime. That's not fair, Max. If you're going to have a dog you have to look after him properly. You know how strongly Dad and I feel about your pets being your responsibility.'

'I know,' Max shrugged. 'Come on, Buddy.'

He opened the door and Buddy bounded out.

'What are you going to do this morning, honey?' Mrs Foster asked Lauren as she put the kettle on.

'I think I'll call Mel and see if we can finish our project,' Lauren replied.

'Well, I'll be in my study if you need me,' Mrs Foster said. She made herself a cup of coffee and went back to work.

Lauren had only just finished her toast when Max came back.

'Did you forget something?' she asked in surprise.

'No, I've finished walking Buddy,' Max replied.

'But that wasn't a long enough walk,' Lauren said, looking at Buddy who was standing hopefully by the door. 'You were only out five minutes.'

'Yeah, but Steven said to come over straight away,' Max said. 'I'll walk Buddy again later. He'll be fine.' He grabbed his skateboard. 'See you, Lauren!'

'Max!' Lauren started to protest, but the door had already banged shut.

Buddy scratched at the door and

whined. Lauren walked over and stroked him. She could take him out for a walk herself but her mum or dad might see her, and then Max would get into trouble for not walking Buddy himself. And now she'd arranged to go to Mel's house to finish off their project. She couldn't leave Mel and Jessica to do it all on their own.

'I'll take you out at lunchtime if Max hasn't walked you properly,' she promised Buddy. She got out a dog chew from the cupboard. Buddy chewed it listlessly.

Lauren felt awful as she let herself out of the house. *Poor Buddy*, she thought as she hurried down the path to Twilight's field.

✶

When Lauren got to Mel's house, the three girls decided to go for a ride in the woods before carrying on with their project.

'We could go to the creek and skim stones,' Mel suggested.

'Cool,' Jessica agreed.

Lauren nodded, but she couldn't get Buddy out of her thoughts. Was he still waiting by the door?

Mel and Jessica tacked up and they rode into the woods. After a while, Mel looked at Lauren. 'You're very quiet. Is everything OK?'

'I'm worried about Buddy,' Lauren admitted. 'Max isn't looking after him properly.' She told the others what was

going on. 'If Mum and Dad find out he
hasn't been walked today they'll be really
mad, and Buddy's so unhappy.'

'Can't you say something to Max?'
Jessica asked.

'I've tried, but he just says Buddy's
happy and I'm worrying about nothing –'

She broke off with a gasp as something
big, black and furry burst out of the

bushes beside them. The three ponies shied in alarm.

'Buddy!' Lauren exclaimed as the Bernese mountain dog skidded to a stop.

'Steady, Sandy!'

Hearing Jessica's alarmed cry, Lauren swung round. Sandy, who was young and easily startled, was racing backwards with her eyes rolling. Jessica had lost her stirrups.

'Hang on, Jess!' Mel cried out as Sandy half-reared up in fear. Jessica grabbed for a handful of mane, but she lost her grip and slipped off Sandy's back, landing on the ground with an uncomfortable thud.

'Whoa, Sandy!' Lauren cried as the palomino pony cantered towards her. She tried to grab Sandy's reins but her fingers closed around thin air.

In a thunder of hooves, Sandy galloped off down a side track into the trees.

'Sandy!' all three girls cried.

Mel looked round and, seeing Jessica still on the floor, leapt off Shadow. 'Jess? Are you OK?'

'I'm fine,' Jessica said, scrambling to her feet. 'But we've got to catch Sandy!'

Buddy trotted towards Shadow. Mel grabbed his collar.

'Twilight's the fastest. I'll go after Sandy!' Lauren said.

'OK,' Mel said.

Tears were streaking down Jessica's face. 'Please catch her, Lauren! *Please!*'

CHAPTER

Seven

Twilight needed no encouragement.
Plunging forward, he galloped in
the same direction as Sandy.

Lauren bent low over his neck, her
heart pounding. Where was Sandy? The
pony could go deeper and deeper into
the woods and get lost completely. Or
maybe she'd find her way on to a road.
Or to the old quarry with its steep

dangerous sides . . .

'Oh, Twilight, we've got to catch her!' Lauren gasped.

Twilight weaved in and out of the trees. The forest grew thicker with every stride. He started to slow down, every so often jumping over a twisted tree root. The trees were too close together for him to gallop safely.

An image of Sandy lying injured filled Lauren's mind. 'Twilight, please! Go as fast as you can!' she begged.

To her surprise, Twilight stopped. Lauren lurched forward on to his neck. 'What are you doing?' Twilight stamped his front hoof and whinnied, and suddenly Lauren knew what he was trying to say. 'It'll be quicker if we fly?'

Twilight nodded.

Lauren glanced round. It was broad daylight and even though they were deep in the heart of the woods it would be really risky to turn Twilight into a unicorn now. Someone might see him. But they had to stop Sandy.

'OK,' she whispered. She quickly said the words of the Turning Spell.

In a second, Twilight was a unicorn.

'Sandy's gone this way,' he said. 'I can see her hoof prints and there are some cream-coloured hairs on that branch over there. She's heading towards the quarry but if I fly fast we might be able to cut her off!'

'Be as quick as you can,' Lauren begged. 'Sandy could really hurt herself!'

Twilight plunged into the air and they flew through the treetops, just skimming the branches.

'There!' Lauren gasped, catching a glimpse of gold through the trees. 'I think I can see her!'

'I'll fly down,' Twilight said.

Lauren saw the deep jagged pit of the quarry as they circled above it and then Twilight swooped to the ground. As he landed on a clear patch of rock, Lauren heard the sound of Sandy's hooves.

'She's coming!'

Sandy burst out of the trees. Her eyes were wide with fear. One of her stirrup leathers had come off and her reins were trailing dangerously around her legs. She was heading straight for the edge of the quarry!

Twilight stepped on to the track and lifted his head. A ray of sunshine filtered through the leaves, lighting up his silver horn and making it sparkle.

With a snort, Sandy slowed down.

Twilight blew out softly and stepped towards her. Bending his head, he let his horn touch her neck. Lauren guessed that he was using his magic power to calm fear. As she watched, the terror gradually faded from Sandy's eyes. Her breathing slowed and she stopped trembling.

Slipping off Twilight's back, Lauren

walked up to the palomino pony. 'It's
OK, girl,' she murmured, reaching out for
the pony's reins.

Sandy whinnied. Twilight nickered
back.

'What's she saying?' Lauren asked.

'She says she was really frightened by
the dog jumping out,' Twilight explained.

'She didn't realize it was Buddy.'

'Oh, Sandy,' Lauren said, smoothing the palomino's white forelock. 'You silly thing. Come on, let's get you back to Mel and Jessica.'

Twilight looked around. 'I guess you should turn me back to a pony first, Lauren. We're near the main track here and someone might see me.'

Lauren said the words of the Undoing Spell and remounted. Then, holding on to Sandy's reins, she led her back through the trees.

Mel and Jessica were waiting where Lauren had left them. Jessica was crying. Mel had one arm around her, with her other hand holding firmly on to Buddy's collar.

'Sandy!' Jessica cried when Lauren appeared with the ponies. She raced over. 'Is she OK?'

'Her reins are broken but she's fine,' Lauren replied, handing Sandy's reins to Jessica and dismounting.

Jessica flung her arms around her pony's neck and hugged her hard. 'Oh, Sandy, I was so worried.'

Sandy nuzzled her.

'She was just startled by Buddy,' Lauren explained. She caught herself quickly. 'I mean, I *think* that's why she galloped off.' She looked at Buddy. 'Buddy, what were you doing in the woods?'

Buddy panted, his tongue hanging out of his mouth. He looked like he was smiling, but Lauren saw him lick his lips and wag just the tip of his tail, two signs that he was feeling confused. 'Come on,' she sighed, stroking his ears. 'I'd better take you home.' She looked at Mel. 'I'll take Buddy back and then come over.'

'OK,' Mel agreed. 'We'll take Shadow and Sandy home.'

Lauren took Twilight's reins over his head and, holding on to Buddy's collar with one hand, she started to trudge home through the woods.

'I guess you were probably trying to find Max,' she said to the dog. 'Well, I hope I can get you back in the house without Mum or Dad seeing that you've been out on your own.'

But as she turned on to the track that led to Twilight's field, her heart sank. Her mum and dad were both near Twilight's stable, calling Buddy's name.

Pulling away from Lauren's hand, Buddy bounded down the track to meet them.

'Hey, where did you find Buddy?' Mr Foster asked in surprise.

'Er, he was in the woods,' Lauren replied. She decided not to mention the fact that Buddy had scared Sandy and made Jessica fall off.

'He escaped from the kitchen,' Mrs Foster said. 'I think he must have pressed the handle down when he was pawing at the door. I saw him go past the study window, towards Twilight's stable. I called him but he didn't stop.' She shook her head. 'It's very strange. He never normally runs off. Max *did* walk him this morning, didn't he, Lauren?'

'Um . . .' Lauren really didn't want to

get Max into trouble. 'Yes. He . . . he *did* take him out.'

Mr Foster seemed to hear the hesitation in her voice. He looked at her shrewdly. 'For a proper walk?'

Lauren felt her cheeks go red. 'Not exactly.'

Mrs Foster looked angry. 'But I *told* Max he wasn't to go to Steven and Leo's until he'd walked Buddy.' She shook her head. 'I'm very cross with him. In fact, I'm going over there right now to bring him home.'

'Oh, Mum, please don't . . .' Lauren protested. She knew how embarrassed Max would be to have their mum turn up to drag him home.

'No, Lauren. Max has gone too far this time. He's been neglecting Buddy ever since he started skateboarding.'

Lauren bit her lip as her mum and dad set off up the path.

'Oh, Twilight,' she whispered. 'Max is in real trouble now.'

Lauren waited with Twilight until she heard her mum's car coming back down the drive. Hurrying up the path, she saw Max getting out of the car. 'It's not fair,' he was shouting. 'Why did I have to come home?'

'You *know* why, Max,' Mrs Foster said, getting out too. 'I asked you to walk Buddy before you went to your friends and you didn't.'

'I did!'

'You didn't take him out for long enough. Lauren told us.'

Max glared at Lauren. 'Thanks, Lauren!'

'Don't take it out on your sister,' Mrs Foster scolded. 'You should have taken Buddy out for a proper walk. He escaped into the woods this morning. Anything could have happened.'

'But nothing did,' Max protested.

Lauren was very glad she hadn't mentioned Sandy's fall. Max and Buddy were in quite enough trouble already.

'That's not the point,' Mrs Foster said. 'Buddy's your responsibility, and if you can't look after him Dad and I are not going to let you keep him. We'll find him another home.'

'No!' Max gasped.

'Mum!' Lauren exclaimed.

'I mean it, Max,' Mrs Foster said firmly. 'I will *not* see an animal neglected.'

'But Buddy's not neglected.' Max

stamped his foot. 'You're not being fair!'

'Go to your bedroom please, Max. We'll talk about this when you've calmed down.'

Max ran into the house, slamming the door behind him.

Lauren stared at her mum. 'Mum, you wouldn't really give Buddy away, would you?'

Mrs Foster ran a hand through her hair. 'I'm sorry, Lauren. I know you love Buddy. I do too. But I can't stand by and see Max make him unhappy.' She sighed. 'I just hope Max gets the message.'

Lauren looked up at her younger brother's bedroom window. *Oh, Max*, she thought. *Please start looking after Buddy properly. Please!*

CHAPTER

Eight

Lauren didn't sleep well that night. She couldn't stop worrying about Max. He had looked after Buddy for the rest of the day, feeding him and brushing him, but he had done it sulkily and Lauren had noticed their mum frowning as she watched him. *If only Buddy could talk to him like Twilight can talk to me,* Lauren thought as she turned over restlessly in bed. *Then he'd be able to tell Max how he feels.*

The next day, Lauren found herself yawning as some of her classmates presented their projects. Even though she loved ponies, it was hard to pay attention when Jade's group began the second talk of the day on how to look after a pony.

'This is a dandy brush,' Jade said, pointing to a picture that was too small for the rest of the class to see. 'And this is a body brush.' She pointed to another picture. 'And this is a curry comb.'

'We've heard all this!' Adam Neil called out. 'David's group did horses this morning!'

'Tell us something different,' said

Adam's friend Simon. 'This is boring!'

'Settle down please, boys,' Mrs Bradshaw, their teacher said. 'Just listen.'

Mel shot Lauren a worried look. Lauren guessed what she was thinking. If people were bored now, how were they going to feel listening to a third presentation about horses? *We've got to make our talk more interesting*, she thought desperately. *But how?*

On the way home from school, Lauren, Max and Mrs Foster stopped at Mrs Fontana's shop so Mrs Foster could collect a book she had ordered.

The doorbell tinkled as they walked in and Walter, Mrs Fontana's terrier, trotted over to meet them.

'Hello,' Mrs Fontana said, appearing from the back of the old-fashioned shop. She was wearing a yellow shawl and her grey hair was held back in a bun. 'You must be here to pick up your book.'

'Yes, please,' Mrs Foster replied.

'Do you have any books on skateboarding, Mrs Fontana?' Max asked.

Mrs Fontana smiled. 'There's some in the children's section. Take a look if you want, Max.'

'Thanks,' Max said. He hurried to the back of the shop.

Mrs Fontana turned to Lauren. 'Lauren, would you mind giving me a hand in the storeroom? I put your mum's book on a high shelf, but my arthritis is playing up today and I would be very grateful if you would help me get it down.'

While her mum browsed, Lauren followed Mrs Fontana to the back of the shop and through a curtain of glass beads that glittered and sparkled. Lauren had never been in the storeroom before. The shelves that lined the narrow walls were packed with books, and there was a small desk in one corner.

'How's Twilight?' Mrs Fontana asked.

'Great,' Lauren replied. 'We discovered that he can untangle thorns with his magic.'

'Ah yes, that's the power he has to make order out of chaos,' Mrs Fontana

nodded. 'Very useful.' She fetched a low
stepladder. 'Your mother's book is on the
second shelf. If you could just reach it
down for me, that would be a great help.'

'Sure.' Lauren climbed up and took the
book down.

Mrs Fontana smiled. 'Thank you, my
dear.'

As she passed her the book, Lauren
noticed how stiff Mrs Fontana's fingers
were. 'Couldn't Twilight use his magic to
cure your arthritis, Mrs Fontana?' she
asked, thinking about how Twilight had
once used his magic to heal cuts on her
hands.

Mrs Fontana shook her head. 'My
arthritis comes from old age. I'm afraid

even unicorn magic can't cure that.'

'Oh,' Lauren said.

Mrs Fontana's blue eyes studied Lauren.
'You look worried about something, my
dear.'

'Two somethings actually,' Lauren
admitted. 'A school project I'm doing,
and Max.' She told Mrs Fontana

everything that had been happening. 'It's awful,' she finished. 'Mum's serious about finding Buddy another home if Max doesn't start looking after him.' She looked hopefully at Mrs Fontana. 'There isn't anything Twilight and I can do, is there?'

'I'm afraid that this is one of those problems – just like my arthritis – that can't be solved by unicorn magic,' Mrs Fontana said. 'It sounds to me that Max has become so caught up in his new hobby that he's forgotten how much Buddy means to him and how much he means to Buddy. But neither you nor Twilight can make him realize that.'

Lauren sighed. 'The thing is, I *know*

Max loves Buddy deep down. He just doesn't seem to understand what he's feeling.' She frowned. 'If only there was some way Buddy could speak to Max, like Twilight can talk to me.'

Mrs Fontana smiled. 'Oh, Lauren. All animals can talk. People just need to listen.'

'What do you mean?' Lauren asked.

Mrs Fontana's eyes crinkled up at the corners. 'You don't need me to explain. If you think about it, my dear, I'm sure you'll work it out on your own. And it might just help you with your problems too.'

Lauren didn't have time to ask Mrs Fontana what she meant before they went back through the curtain into the shop.

Lauren's mum and Max were standing by the counter. 'We'd better get going,' said Mrs Foster.

Mrs Fontana rang up the purchase on the till. 'See you again soon,' she called as they left.

'Bye, Mrs Fontana,' Lauren replied. She was still thinking about what Mrs Fontana had said in the storeroom. '*All animals can talk. People just need to listen.*' *What did she mean? Animals couldn't talk. Well, apart from Twilight, and that was only because he was a unicorn.*

'I just don't get it,' she said as she groomed Twilight a little while later. 'Animals can't talk. What did Mrs

Fontana mean?'

Twilight stamped his hoof. Just then,
Lauren noticed a patch of mud on his
tummy just where his girth would go.
She started to brush at it quickly. Twilight
threw his head up and swished his tail.

'What's the matter?' Lauren asked. 'Was
I being too rough? Sorry.' She began to
brush more carefully, this time using
smooth gentle strokes.

Twilight relaxed and Lauren smiled.
Sometimes she didn't need him to be a
unicorn to understand what he was
saying.

Her eyes widened.

'Of course! That's what Mrs Fontana
means!'

Twilight looked round at her.

'She *wasn't* saying that animals can speak to people like you talk to me when you're a unicorn. She meant that animals can communicate with people in other ways. Like when you put your ears back, I know that means you're unhappy, and when you stamp your hoof, you're impatient.'

Twilight tossed his head.

A thought struck Lauren. 'And it's not just ponies, is it? Other animals can talk to people too. Maybe that's what Mrs Fontana meant about Max. If he can watch Buddy closely and understand what he's saying, he'll find it easier to look after him —' She broke off.

She'd just had the perfect idea for the school project!

CHAPTER
Nine

'What do you think?' Lauren asked, looking at Mel and Jessica a little while later. 'How about we do a project on how ponies talk to us?'

Mel and Jessica were staring at her as if they thought she'd gone crazy.

'But Lauren,' Jessica said, 'ponies don't talk.'

'They do!' Lauren insisted. 'Sure, they

don't open their mouths and speak
words, but they tell us what they're
thinking by the way they move their ears
and heads and tails. I think we should do
our project on how ponies –' she
searched for the right word – 'how they
communicate.'

Mel and Jessica still didn't look
convinced.

'Watch.' Lauren led Twilight over to
where Shadow was tied up. Shadow
pricked his ears and the two ponies
touched noses. 'They're saying hello.
Breathing out through their nostrils is
their way of greeting each other – or us.'
She walked up to Shadow and he
obligingly lifted his head and blew on to

her face. 'See, he's saying hello to me!'

'I guess so. I hadn't really thought about it as talking,' Mel said.

'I know, but that's what it is,' Lauren said. 'And I think the rest of our class would be really interested if we did our project on this.'

Jessica nodded. 'We could still use our posters and things, but if we did this as well it would be loads better than just doing another talk on how to look after a horse.'

'Yes,' Mel agreed. 'I know, how about we make a *video* of our ponies and show it to the class?'

'That's a great idea!' Lauren exclaimed. 'We could film the ponies doing different

things and explain to the class what
they're saying with their body language.
We could even take some regular photos
and get the class to guess what moods the
ponies are in each picture.'

The three girls looked at each other
excitedly.

'No one would be bored if we did
that,' Mel said. 'I'll go and ask Mum if I
can borrow our video camera.'

Luckily, Mrs Cassidy agreed and the three
girls set about filming Shadow, Sandy and
Twilight. Twilight was wonderful. He
swished his tail when Lauren groomed
his tummy, and put his ears forward and
whickered when Lauren walked up to

him. He tossed his head when Lauren did his girth up too tight, and stamped his hoof when she rattled his feed bucket.

'It's like he understands what we want!' Mel exclaimed.

Lauren hid a grin. There were some *definite* advantages to Twilight being a unicorn!

The girls worked until the sun was

setting and it was time for Lauren to ride
home.

'I'll ask Mum to bring me back as soon
as I've fed Twilight and turned him out
in the field,' she promised.

'OK. We'll put Sandy and Shadow away
and start looking at the video,' said Mel.

When Lauren reached Twilight's stable
she saw Max practising on his skateboard.
He was jumping in the air and trying to
turn the board under his feet.
Remembering that she'd been meaning
to talk to him about Buddy, Lauren
untacked Twilight and went to the gate.
'Max,' she called. 'Can I talk to you for a
minute?'

'Not now,' Max replied. 'Steven and

Leo are coming over tomorrow and I want to be able to do this kick flip perfectly.' He turned his skateboard round and tried again.

Lauren hesitated. *I'll talk to him later*, she decided, and she went back to Twilight.

But when Lauren finally got back from Mel's house that night, it was eight thirty and Max had already gone to bed.

I guess I'll just have to wait till the morning, she decided. Kicking off her boots, she headed upstairs to take a shower.

The next morning, Max was already up and practising on his skateboard when

Lauren went outside to give Twilight his breakfast.

'Max!' Lauren called, waving to him. 'Come over here.'

'I can't,' Max replied. 'I'm practising.'

'I wanted to talk to you about Buddy,' Lauren said, going over to him. 'I don't think you understand what he's thinking a lot of the time, and that makes it hard for you to look after him.'

Max looked confused.

'Think about when he wags his tail,' Lauren persisted. 'Sometimes it means he's happy, but sometimes it means he's confused or worried. It depends *how* he wags his tail. There are other things as well, like how he pricks his ears and if he's panting or not. They're all ways he tries to talk to you.'

Max didn't look convinced. 'Yeah, right.' He got on his skateboard again.

'Max, this is important!' Lauren protested. 'I really can help you to understand Buddy better –'

'Some other time,' Max said, and he began to skate away from her.

Lauren watched him go, feeling frustrated, before heading back to the tack room. She needed to feed Twilight and get ready for school. Butterflies fluttered in her stomach at the thought of presenting their project that afternoon.

She mixed Twilight's feed and took it to the paddock. 'I hope the other kids like all the stuff we've done about horses,' she told him.

He lifted his head and snorted reassuringly. Bits of grain fell on to Lauren's jeans, but she didn't care. She knew he was just trying to tell her that everything would be fine. She hugged him.

'Thanks, Twilight,' she said, feeling better. 'I'll come and see you as soon as I get home to tell you all about it.'

She gave him a kiss, then climbed over the gate and hurried back to the house.

CHAPTER

Ten

Lauren, Jessica and Mel were the very last group to present their project. The previous talk had been on stick insects and even Mrs Bradshaw had looked as if she was having trouble staying awake.

'Well, it's time for the last presentation,' she announced, sounding relieved. 'Lauren, Mel, Jessica, would you come up please?'

'Not another talk on horses!' Adam complained.

'Oh no,' Simon groaned.

'Well, it's not just a talk about how to look after a horse,' said Lauren as she walked up to the front with Mel and Jessica following. 'It's about how horses communicate.'

'Yes,' Jessica backed her up. 'And how people can tell what horses are thinking.'

The class looked more interested.

'OK,' Mrs Bradshaw said. 'Now, you told me you'd like to use the video recorder. It's all set up, so when you're ready, you can start.'

'Cool! We get to watch TV,' Adam said, looking more cheerful.

Lauren exchanged looks with Mel and Jessica. They had agreed that she would start. Taking a deep breath, she smiled at the class. 'Our project is called "Animals can talk, if only people listen". We're going to show you how ponies communicate and how easy it is to understand what they're trying to say.' She glanced at Mel. 'Mel, can you start the video please?'

To Lauren, Jessica and Mel's relief, their talk was a great success. The whole class listened while they showed them the video and talked about what the ponies were doing. Then Jessica gave out the photos they'd printed and they split the

class into groups to guess the ponies'
moods.

There was a picture of Twilight with
his ears back, one of Sandy pawing the
ground, one of Shadow with his ears
pricked in excitement and a picture of
Twilight nuzzling Lauren affectionately.

Even Adam and Simon joined in and
called out suggestions. Mel finished by

holding up her posters. Everyone loved Mel's cartoons and Mrs Bradshaw said she would stick them up on the classroom wall.

'That was a fascinating project!' she said when the girls had finished. 'You should be very proud of yourselves – and your ponies. They posed beautifully for the photos and it was clear exactly what they were saying.'

'It was cool!' Adam called out.

Someone started to clap and the whole class joined in. Lauren, Mel and Jessica blushed and exchanged pleased smiles.

Just then the bell rang. With the sound of the applause still ringing in their ears, the three girls headed for the cloakroom.

'I can't believe it went so well!' Mel exclaimed.

'You were great, Lauren,' Jessica said. 'You explained everything perfectly.'

Lauren grinned. She felt proud but also very relieved. It was over and it had been a success. She couldn't wait to get home and tell Twilight all about it!

When she went into the schoolyard she was surprised to see Steven and Leo standing with Max; then she remembered that they were coming home with him to play.

All the way back to the farm, the boys talked about skateboarding.

As soon as Mrs Foster pulled up

outside the farmhouse, Max jumped out
of the car. 'The ramps are this way!'

'Max!' Mrs Foster said. 'Maybe Steven
and Leo want to get a drink first.'

'We're fine, thanks,' Steven said politely.
'Aren't we, Leo?'

Leo nodded. 'We'd really love to see the
skateboard stuff, Mrs Foster.'

'OK,' Mrs Foster said, smiling. 'Off
you go!'

The boys grabbed their skateboards and helmets and hurried off. Mrs Foster turned to Lauren. 'Steven and Leo are nice, aren't they?'

Lauren nodded. 'Yeah, though a bit skateboard mad. I thought Max was bad enough!'

Mrs Foster headed for the house. 'Are you coming in?'

'I'll just go see Twilight first,' Lauren replied. She ran down the track towards Twilight's paddock. He was waiting at the gate.

'Hi, boy,' Lauren said, patting him. 'The project was great! Everyone loved the video.'

On the other side of the field, the boys

were already on their skateboards. 'Watch this!' Max called. He jumped in the air and flipped his board.

'Way to go!' Steven said.

Max looked very proud. 'I can do a kick flip after coming down a ramp, too.'

'Are you sure, Max?' Leo said. 'That's really difficult.'

'Yeah,' Steven said doubtfully. 'You haven't been skating that long.'

'Watch!' Max insisted. He skated up to the highest ramp.

Just then, there was the sound of thundering paws. Lauren turned to see Buddy charging down the path from the house. He galloped straight towards Max just as he started coming down the ramp, his face frowning in concentration.

Max looked up in alarm as Buddy woofed, and his skateboard wobbled. Max's arms flailed wildly, but it was too late and the skateboard flipped over.

'Oh no!' Lauren gasped as Max crashed to the ground. She ran to the fence. 'Are you OK, Max?'

Buddy jumped on top of Max, his tail wagging like mad.

'I'm fine. Get off, Buddy!' Max shouted. 'You stupid dumb dog!' He clambered to his feet. His cheeks were bright red with embarrassment.

'Are you sure you're all right?' Steven said hurrying over to him. 'That was a bad fall.'

'It was a really difficult move to try,'
Leo agreed. 'Especially since you haven't
been skateboarding that long.'

Lauren saw tears of humiliation in her
brother's eyes. 'I'd have been fine if it
hadn't been for Buddy. I only fell off
because of him.' He turned on Buddy. 'I
hate you! You always wreck everything.
Well, I hope Mum and Dad do give you
away after all!'

With that he turned and ran into the
house.

There was an awkward silence. Buddy
sat down and whined.

'Oh, Buddy,' Lauren said, climbing the
fence. Buddy came trotting over to her
and thrust his nose into her hand.

Steven looked at his younger brother. 'You shouldn't have said that, Leo. You made it sound like Max was just a little kid. He might have managed the jump if he hadn't been distracted by the dog.'

Leo looked awkward. 'I just meant it was a difficult jump for a beginner.' He looked at Lauren. 'I didn't mean to upset Max.'

Lauren sighed. 'Don't worry. I think he was just embarrassed about falling off.'

Steven walked over to her. 'Is this your dog?'

'No, he's Max's,' Lauren replied. 'Hasn't Max ever told you about him?'

'No,' Steven replied. 'But then we always just talk about skateboarding. He stroked Buddy's head. 'Hi there, fella.'

Buddy's tail thumped on the ground.

Leo started petting him too. Buddy
jumped up and pushed against Leo's legs,
almost knocking him over. Leo laughed.

'What should we do about Max?'
Steven said.

'I don't think there's anything you *can*
do,' Lauren said. 'It's best to give him a
chance to calm down. I'll go see him in a
minute.'

'I guess we should go home then,'
Steven said to Leo. 'It doesn't seem right
to practise on Max's ramps without him.'

'Will your mum or dad be home?'
Lauren asked.

'Mum will,' Steven replied. 'Tell Max to

come and find us if he wants. He can
bring his skateboard over.'

The two boys gave Buddy one last pat
and set off. Buddy made as if to follow
them but Lauren grabbed his collar. 'No,
you don't, Buddy.'

Buddy whimpered and tried to pull
after the boys.

Lauren sighed. She knew she should go see how Max was. She walked up to the house with Buddy. When she got to the back door she stopped. 'Maybe you should wait here, Buddy. I'm not sure Max will want to see you at the moment.' She could still hear Max's words ringing in her ears. *I hate you! I hope Mum and Dad do give you away.* She was sure Max had only said those things because he'd been feeling humiliated. But what sort of mood would he be in now?

As she reached the top of the stairs she heard the sound of Max crying.

'Max?' Lauren said, pushing his bedroom door open. 'Max? Are you OK?'

Her brother was lying on his bed. 'Go away!'

'Max, don't cry. There's nothing to be upset about.'

'Yes there is. Steven and Leo just think I'm a dorky little kid.'

'No they don't,' Lauren protested, going and sitting on his bed.

'They do. I fell off my skateboard.'

'So? I'm sure everyone falls off,' Lauren told him. 'It's like horse riding. The important thing is that you get back up and try again.'

'I guess,' Max muttered. He sniffed. 'I just wish Leo and Steven hadn't been there. I feel so stupid.'

'Don't worry,' Lauren said. 'Leo and

Steven won't care about you falling off. They're your friends. It's like Jessica and Mel. They don't laugh at me if I make mistakes on Twilight. They make me feel better.'

There was a silence as Max thought about what she'd said. 'Really?'

'Really,' Lauren told him.

The tears started to dry on Max's face. 'Where are Leo and Steven now?'

'They went home. I think they felt a bit awkward,' Lauren replied. 'But they told me to tell you to go round and see them. They said to bring your skateboard.'

'So they *do* still want to be friends with me?' Max asked.

Lauren nodded.

Max looked relieved. 'I'll go over right now,' he said, getting up and heading for the door.

'Max,' Lauren said. He stopped and looked at her. 'You weren't very nice to Buddy just now,' she told him. 'He didn't mean any harm. He was just excited to see you. If you'd gone to see him when you got home, he wouldn't have come racing out like that.'

Max hesitated. 'I guess.' He looked rather shamefaced. 'I didn't really mean those things I said, you know.'

'I know, but it upset Buddy,' Lauren told him. 'He couldn't understand why you were shouting at him just for saying hello.'

Max bit his lip. 'All right. I'll tell him everything's OK. Where is he?'

'Outside,' Lauren replied.

They went down to the kitchen.

'Buddy! Here, boy!' Max called, opening the door.

But Buddy didn't appear.

'Buddy! Where are you?' Max called again.

Lauren fetched Buddy's tin bowl and banged it. It was a sound that usually made Buddy come running. But not this time.

'Where is he?' Max frowned.

'I don't know,' said Lauren, starting to feel worried. 'I left him here.'

'It's not like Buddy to wander off,' Max said. 'Maybe it's because I shouted at him.' His eyes widened and his face went pale. 'Oh, Lauren!' he exclaimed. 'Do you think he's run away?'

CHAPTER

Eleven

L auren stared at her brother. 'Run
away?'

'I said I hated him!' Max burst out. 'I
said I didn't want him any more. He
might have thought I meant it!' He ran
outside. 'Buddy!' he called. 'Come back. I
didn't mean any of those things!'

But still no Buddy.

Tears started to well in Max's eyes.

'Buddy! *Buddy!*'

Lauren felt her heart beat faster. 'We'd better tell Mum,' she said. 'Come on!'

Mrs Foster was very concerned to hear that Buddy had disappeared. 'He didn't even come back when you banged his food bowl?' she asked Lauren.

Lauren shook her head.

'I said I hated him, Mum. He's run away and it's all my fault!' Max said, tears running down his face.

'Calm down, Max,' Mrs Foster said. 'Buddy wouldn't run away just because of something you said.'

'I bet he would!' Max said, his words coming out in a sob. 'He thinks I don't want him, but I do!'

'Do you want me to go and look in the woods with Twilight?' Lauren offered.

'Thanks, honey,' Mrs Foster said. 'I'll tell your dad and we'll search here on the farm.'

Lauren gave Max a quick hug. 'We'll find Buddy. Don't worry!'

She raced down the path. If she could just get Twilight into the woods and turn him into a unicorn, she could use his magic to find out where Buddy was. When Twilight touched his horn to rose quartz he could see anyone he wanted, *and* see where they were.

Twilight whinnied when he saw her.

'Buddy's disappeared,' Lauren told him.

'You didn't see him go, did you?'

Twilight shook his head.

'We've got to find him,' Lauren said.
'Let's go to the clearing in the woods so
you can use your magic to look for him!'

She put Twilight's bridle on but didn't
bother with his saddle. 'Come on!' she
said, leading him out of the field and
swinging herself on to his back.

As Twilight cantered into the woods,
Lauren clung to his mane. Riding him
bareback was much easier when he was
in his magical shape and he had unicorn
magic to keep her on!

Twilight leapt over a tree root in the
path.

'Steady, boy!' Lauren gasped.

Just then, she heard the faint sound of
barking. 'That sounds like Buddy!' she
exclaimed.

She looked and looked, but the trees
were so thick she couldn't see anything.
She hesitated. Should they follow the
noise or keep going to the clearing?

Woof! Woof! The bark was faint but it

definitely sounded like Buddy. Twilight pulled towards the trees.

Lauren made up her mind. 'OK, Twilight. If you think it's Buddy, let's go that way.'

Twilight started to weave in and out of the trees as the path faded away. Ducking under branches, Lauren felt her heart pounding. Where was Buddy?

She remembered how he'd spooked Sandy and made her run off. What if he caused another accident? What if he was in an accident himself? An icy shiver ran down her spine.

The woofing was coming from the edge of the woods where there were houses – and a road.

'Hurry, Twilight!' Lauren urged, feeling sick with worry.

Suddenly Twilight stopped. There was a low fence ahead marking out the boundary between the woods and the gardens behind the houses. But a deep thicket of blackberry bushes blocked the way to the fence.

'Oh no!' Lauren exclaimed in dismay.

She heard another bark. It seemed to come from just the other side of the fence. *Oh Buddy*, Lauren thought desperately. *Please don't be in trouble!*

'We'll have to go back,' she told Twilight. 'We can't get through this way.' But to her surprise Twilight didn't move when she pulled his mane.

'Twilight!' she exclaimed.

Twilight tossed up his head and stamped his hoof.

Lauren frowned. She had a feeling he was trying to tell her something. But what?

Twilight pushed at the bushes with his nose.

In a flash, Lauren realized what he'd been trying to say. *His magic powers!* He could try to use them to untangle the blackberry branches! 'You want me to turn you into a unicorn?'

Twilight nodded.

Lauren looked around. She was desperate to get to Buddy but it was very risky to turn Twilight into a unicorn in broad daylight. Still, the trees were really thick between her and the houses. She decided to take the risk.

Scrambling off Twilight's back, she said the magic words.

In a flash, Twilight turned into a unicorn. 'I can use my magic to try and clear a path by untangling the brambles,' he explained.

'Do you think it will work?' Lauren asked. These bushes were much thicker than the place where the squirrel had been trapped.

Twilight looked determined, and his

horn glowed even brighter. 'I'll try!'

He lowered his horn to the branches
and, sure enough, the briars started to
unravel! Twilight took a step forward,
touching his horn to the next tangle of
branches. Little by little, a narrow
pathway appeared.

'You're doing it, Twilight!' Lauren cried
in delight.

As the last brambles unwound
themselves, Lauren's impatience got the
better of her and she forced her way
through. Ignoring the scratches on her
arms, she ran to the fence and peered over.

'Twilight! It *is* Buddy!'

The fence bordered a long garden with
a large house at the far end. Near the

house was a hard tennis court with various pieces of skateboarding equipment on it — a ramp, a quarter pipe and several jumps. Two boys were rolling around on skateboards and, playing with them and woofing excitedly, was Buddy!

Lauren felt a wave of relief rush through her. Buddy was safe. He wasn't on the road and he wasn't in trouble.

'It's Leo and Steven,' Twilight said, joining Lauren at the fence. 'This must be their house.'

'I wonder what Buddy's doing here?' Lauren said.

'Maybe he got bored waiting outside your house and decided to follow Leo and Steven home?' Twilight suggested.

Lauren nodded. She felt trembly with relief. 'I'm so glad he's not in trouble. Should we go into the garden and get him? The fence is only low. You could easily jump it.'

'OK,' Twilight agreed. 'But you'd better change me back first.'

Lauren grinned. 'Yes. I think I'd better.' Steven and Leo seemed to like dogs but she had a feeling they'd be a bit surprised to see a real live unicorn in their garden!

She said the Undoing Spell and cantered Twilight up to the fence. He leapt over it easily.

The boys looked round. Seeing Lauren and Twilight, Buddy barked joyfully and ran over. 'Oh, Buddy,' Lauren said, getting off Twilight and hugging him. 'We've been so worried about you!'

'How did you get here?' Steven asked in surprise.

'I jumped over the fence,' Lauren said. 'I was looking for Buddy in the woods and I heard him barking.'

'But what about the blackberry bushes?' Steven asked. 'They're really thick on the other side of the fence.'

'Oh, I found a way through,' Lauren said quickly. 'How long has Buddy been here?'

'He arrived about ten minutes ago,' said Leo. 'He came trotting into the garden as if he wanted to come and play with us.'

'Max will be so pleased to know he's safe,' Lauren said. 'I should go and tell him Buddy's here.'

'Or I could ring Max and let him know right away,' Steven suggested.

'Yes please!' Lauren replied.

Steven set off towards the house. Leo stroked Twilight. 'He's lovely.'

'Thanks,' Lauren smiled. 'Do you like animals?'

'I love them,' Leo said. 'Steven does too. We used to have a dog, a golden retriever called Jake, but he died last year. It's been really weird without him.' He brightened up slightly. 'But Mum and Dad say we can get another dog now we've moved to the country. Maybe it could be friends with Buddy.'

'Yeah!' Lauren exclaimed. 'That would be great!'

Buddy wagged his tail and woofed.

Five minutes later, there was the sound of a car on the drive and Max came tearing into the garden. 'Buddy!'

Buddy charged over to him. He

stopped too late and almost sent Max flying, but Max didn't care. He flung his arms around the dog. 'Buddy, I'm so glad you're all right. I promise I'll never be mean to you again.'

Buddy licked his face. 'Yuk!' Max exclaimed, but then he laughed and hugged him even harder.

Mrs Foster came round the corner. 'Hello, Steven. Hello, Leo. I'm very glad you found Buddy.'

'Well, actually he found us,' Steven said.

'Whichever way round it was, I'm just glad he's safe,' Mrs Foster replied. She looked at Lauren. 'You did well to track him down.'

Lauren smiled. 'Twilight helped.'

Twilight snorted proudly.

'You know, sometimes I'm sure Twilight can understand every word you say,' Mrs Foster commented.

Lauren stroked Twilight to hide her grin.

'Come on, Max. Shall we take Buddy home?' said Mrs Foster.

Lauren saw Leo's and Steven's faces fall. 'Couldn't Max and Buddy stay here for a while?' she said.

'Yes please!' Steven exclaimed.

'But I haven't got my skateboard,' Max said.

'That's fine. We can play with Buddy instead,' said Steven.

Buddy woofed.

'We love dogs!' Steven told Max. 'We're going to get a puppy soon.'

'We'll be able to take our new dog and Buddy for walks together,' Leo added.

Max looked delighted. 'Cool!'

'Come on,' urged Steven. 'I bet Buddy will love running up and down the ramps and doing the jumps.'

'I'll come back in an hour,' Mrs Foster told Max.

'OK. See you later, Mum!' Max called, and he ran off after Leo and Steven with Buddy bounding around them.

'See you at home, Lauren,' said Mrs Foster.

Lauren nodded and got back on Twilight. The boys were charging about

the skateboard course with Buddy beside
them. Lauren watched for a moment.

'I'm glad it's all worked out OK,' she
murmured to Twilight.

He whickered in agreement.

'Come on,' she said softly. 'Let's go
home.'

As they started up the garden, Max ran
over. 'Lauren? Thanks for finding Buddy.
I'm never going to be mean to him ever
again.'

'Good,' Lauren smiled.

Max hesitated. 'And . . . um . . . you
know what you were saying this
morning, about how I can learn to tell
what Buddy's thinking, by looking at his
tail and ears? Well, will you help me learn

that stuff?' He looked hopefully at
Lauren. 'I'd really like to know what
Buddy's saying.'

'Of course I'll help you,' Lauren told
him.

'Thanks. I want to make him happy,'
Max vowed. 'When I thought he'd run
away, it was awful.'

Lauren glanced across to where Buddy
was playing with Leo and Steven. 'He
sure looks happy now.'

Max grinned. 'He does, doesn't he? I'll
see you later, Lauren!' And with that, he
ran back to join the others.

Lauren rode Twilight towards the fence.
He cleared it easily again.

As the trees closed around them,

Lauren slipped off his back and said the
Turning Spell. With a purple flash,
Twilight turned into a unicorn.

'We did it,' he said in delight. 'We
found Buddy!'

'Yes, and it looks like Max isn't going
to find it so lonely looking after him
from now on.' Lauren leant her head

against Twilight's neck and breathed in his warm sweet smell. 'Thanks for helping, Twilight.'

'That's OK.' Twilight nuzzled her.

'I love you, Twilight,' Lauren whispered, hugging him hard.

They stood there for a moment, and then Lauren said the Undoing Spell. Twilight turned back into a pony and, climbing on to his back, Lauren rode him through the trees.

As the dusk gathered around them and Twilight's hooves thudded on the forest floor, Lauren felt as if they were lost in their own private little world. She looked at Twilight's pricked ears. She knew she'd love him even if he couldn't talk, even if he was just a regular pony.

All ponies are special, she thought to herself. *And they can all talk to us if we just listen.*

She stroked Twilight's neck and smiled. All ponies *were* special, but unicorns were very special indeed.

My Secret Unicorn

When Lauren recites a secret spell, her pony Twilight
turns into a beautiful unicorn with magical powers!
Together Lauren and Twilight learn how to
use their magic to help their friends.

The Magic Spell
Linda Chapman

Dreams Come True
Linda Chapman

Flying High
Linda Chapman

Starlight Surprise
Linda Chapman

Stronger Than Magic
Linda Chapman

A Special Friend
Linda Chapman

A Touch of Magic
Linda Chapman

Twilight Magic
Linda Chapman

Friends Forever
Linda Chapman

Rising Star
Linda Chapman

Look out for more **My Secret Unicorn** adventures

My Secret Unicorn

Most of the time, Twilight looks like an ordinary grey pony, but when Lauren says the words of a spell he transforms into a magical unicorn and together they can fly all over the world . . .

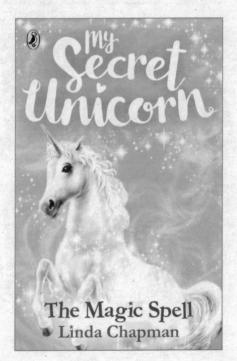

Look out for more My Secret Unicorn adventures

My Secret Unicorn

Lauren's nervous about starting a new school and making new friends. Can Twilight's magical powers help?

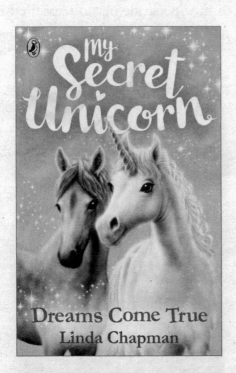

My Secret Unicorn
Dreams Come True
Linda Chapman

Look out for more **My Secret Unicorn** adventures

Cover illustrations © Andrew Farley

My Secret Unicorn

Lauren's friend Jessica is finding life at home difficult. Lauren and Twilight want to help her but can they persuade her to trust them?

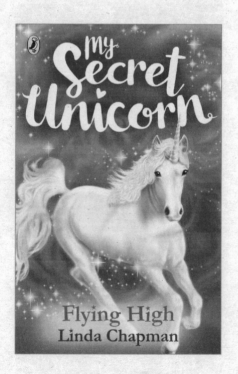

My Secret Unicorn
Flying High
Linda Chapman

Look out for more **My Secret Unicorn** adventures